THE MONKEY'S JOURNAL

AND OTHER SHORT STORIES

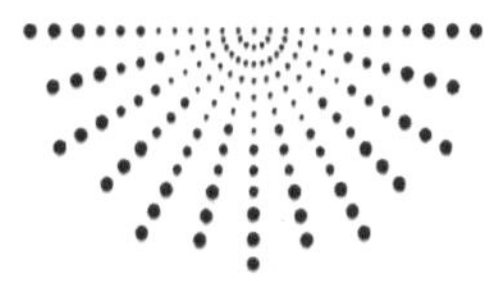

STEPHANNIE TALLENT

For more information, contact: stephannie@stephannietallent.com

First e-Book edition October 2021

E-Book ISBN: 978-1-942655-29-9
Print ISBN: 978-1-942655-30-5

www.stephannietallent.com

To PH: You'll always be my baby brother!

CONTENTS

INTRODUCTION

Travel from 1930s Appalachia to modern day California in this collection of fantasy short stories.

In *Magic of Long and Lightning*, what if the book women, those intrepid librarians delivering materials to their charges on horseback, brought more than mundane knowledge to their patrons?

Gancanaghs, or love talkers, are a type of Irish fairy whose raison d'être is seduction. In *Victory Girl*, tomboy Ruthie realizes what she truly desires.

The Songs of Their Lives was inspired by murder ballads: those tales of deceit, betrayal, and death. But Darla is writing a new ending to those songs.

Who hasn't lost pets over the years? The pain of losing them is the price for the joy they give us. Different people have different ways of remembering their beloved cats and dogs and other creatures (and trust me, as a vet, I've seen a variety of choices). *The Life of Stuffed Toys* looks at one (albeit offbeat) way (yes, different methods of pet taxidermy are available).

Down to the Heart is a triathlon fairytale. And though I haven't had *quite* the same experiences, there's a lot of me in Jennifer.

The Monkey's Journal is about books and cats and wishes and guilt: my take on the Monkey's Paw.

I hope you enjoy this collection.

MAGIC OF SONG AND LIGHTNING

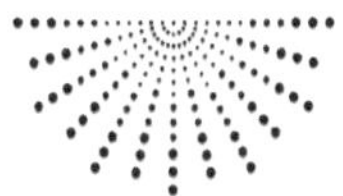

Hoofbeats a-tripping along the rocky lane
Children, children, the bookwoman's come again

The rain started slow, plopping thick drops of coldness down the back of Betty's neck, startling her out of her travel song. She wore a dark gray felted fedora, but the edges were worn and soft and couldn't fend off the plonking raindrops. Her long brown hair was bundled up under the hat, pins all askew, wisps hanging out all over and channeling the rain down under the collar of her long-sleeved white cotton shirt.

She'd ridden seventeen miles that day, and her circuit was almost done. One more homestead, a cabin up the top of the next ridge. After that she would head three miles to the Baptist church in Crooked Creek Hollow, where she could stable her mud-brown gelding Jessie and get herself a hot meal and a good night's sleep.

Just rotten luck the summer monsoon thunderheads had rushed in with the setting sun. The air smelled hot, oil on a cast iron griddle, and she kept an eye out for lightning. No travel song could keep the two of them safe from a stray bolt of lightning.

Her song magic best focused on small things. Keeping Jessie's shoes free of pebbles. Guiding an unfriendly eye past the two of them. Sparking a fire in spite of rain-damp tinder.

Jessie barely flicked a long hairy ear at the rain. Nothing much troubled him. He had a long easy stride like riding a rocking chair, and a sweet disposition to match. Fifteen years he'd been her partner, since she was just thirteen herself, entranced with the gangly awkward colt who'd chosen her, an equally awkward gangly girl.

Blanche, the bookwoman the next county over, scoffed at his pedestrian looks, laughing at his saucer-sized feet, but Betty wouldn't trade Jessie for Blanche's dainty warmblood mare even if you tossed in ten dollars to seal the bargain. Blanche put far too much importance on looks over function, far as Betty was concerned.

Could be why Blanche was divorced and working as a bookwoman, as opposed to still married to that fancy businessman in Louisville.

Betty didn't have a man, but that was by choice, not bad decisions.

The rain fell harder, zinging against her face, and a bolt of lightning hit a tall black oak up on the ridge ahead. Close to the Ashcraft cabin, she reckoned. The thunder pounded against her eardrums.

Darn it all, she wished she could just turn around. But she had to get the scrapbook—a collection of journal entries, dried plant cuttings, and spells—she carried in her worn saddlebags, nestled in amongst the other books donated by the county, to the Ashcraft daughter, Evie.

The girl was growing into her witchy powers, and she needed guidance.

Guidance Evie's momma *would've* given her, had she not been murdered a decade ago, strung up from a rock maple that never produced syrup after that, just thick sweet poison that dripped and pooled around its roots, warning everyone away.

Guidance her daddy couldn't give her, though he loved his daughter dearly, dearly enough he confessed his daughter's powers to Betty, knowing that confession could be their death warrant.

The confession was unnecessary. Betty had two good eyes and a brain to match, as well as power of her own.

The skinny blonde girl, just turned fourteen, green eyes sparking with curiosity and smarts, had tried to damp down her magic last time Betty came through on circuit. Didn't work. The little fox cub cowering under the girl's threadbare floursack skirts was a dead give-away. Every young witch found her familiar before any other power.

Betty would've intervened regardless, even if the girl's daddy hadn't asked. Folks up here in the East Kentucky hills were suspicious, and that suspicion would light upon Rose Ashcraft's little girl soon enough. People were hungry, starving, and there was no work anywhere. Not now, not for years, and likely not for the next several years.

People looking for a reason for bad fortune generally found one, even if it wasn't the right reason.

Never mind the county went to an even deeper hell in a handbasket, once Rose and her nurturing magics were gone from this sorry world.

And then there were folks who knew how to suck the power out of a young untrained witch, to steal it and use it for themselves. The type of folks who the normal folks rightly would be suspicious of. The type of folks that maybe did deserve what had happened to Rose, though Rose herself certainly hadn't.

Evie needed to learn how to hide her powers, and the scrapbook Betty had carefully pieced together would teach her.

Most scrapbooks consisted of quilting patterns, or canning recipes, or the news from the past couple months, all carefully pieced from newspapers and magazines donated to the library and from books too worn out to circulate anymore.

Betty had disguised this scrapbook, her treatise on learning magic, as a simple gardening book. It still could be used for that. Plant your beans with corn and such.

Another flash of lightning and the blast of thunder. The rain whipped around her, turning the rocky path up the hillside to the Ashcraft cabin into a slick morass of mud and sharp stones. Her soaked shirt clung to her ribs and she shivered. She just didn't have enough meat on her bones to keep her warm. Too much magic spent, not enough food eaten. She didn't think she could even carry a tune to calm the weather. Couldn't spare the energy or heat.

Jessie ducked his head down, shaking his thick mane, and trudged uphill, his big feet finding solid purchase. He knew the way after two years of this circuit.

Betty hoped Ashcraft could brew her some hot chamomile tea with honey. She had some sweet feed she could give Jessie, a treat he'd well earned, while she warmed herself up.

The loose wisps of her hair stuck straight out from her head, and Jessie's mane was a bottle brush, thick hairs standing up stiff.

A flash blasted her eyes. She and Jessie were knocked backwards, Jessie scrambling for purchase in the mud and Betty half out of the saddle, hanging off to the side, even as thunder echoed around them, ringing her ears.

She hauled herself back upright and stroked his neck, calming him down. Calming herself down, too. All she could see was spots dancing in front of her eyes, and she figured it was the same for Jessie.

Any other horse would've bolted straight back down the mountain, breaking both their necks.

They stayed still for a good minute, until Betty could finally see clearly.

Lightning had struck a third time, splitting the dead chestnut at the base of the rutted path leading the final stretch up to the cabin, not forty feet ahead. The tree was on fire, bright blue flames licking up at the gunmetal gray sky. The rain dowsed the fire soon enough, but Betty didn't like the look of it: that witchy blue at the center, white at the edges—it wasn't just a natural fire.

Something else was riding the storm. Something with a serious hurt on for her.

———

MAGIC, no matter what superstitious folks thought, wasn't intrinsically bad.

One of two things made it black: how you powered your magic, and what you did with it.

Use your own self to power it, and don't hurt anyone, leastwise not anyone who's not aiming to hurt you first, and you fall on the side of the angels.

Betty rode the last fifty yards to the small log cabin, hitching Jessie to the lower beam of the front porch railing. She picked her way through the mud and up the front steps and banged on the door, humming under her breath. She scraped her boots on the tattered rope rug, wincing at the smears of mud. She knocked again.

Evie answered, her bottle green eyes bright with tears. A tomato red handprint marked her cheek. Her fox cub, nearly full grown now, all gangly with a bushy tail, had the same wide-eyed look of fear as he squeezed out past Evie's legs and cowered next to Betty, hunkering down in the mud from her boots.

Who'd hurt the girl?

"She said she would kill Daddy if'n I didn't go with her," Evie whispered, her voice nearly swallowed by the rattle of rain on the rough shingles of the cabin's roof.

"I won't let anyone hurt you or your daddy," promised Betty.

"And what will you do to stop me, Betty Walker?" a soft sweet voice called.

Blanche? Blanche Devens?

"Step aside, Evie," Betty said. "Trust me."

Blanche stood next to the dining room table across the main room, cupping something in one palm, clutching a bloodstained knife with the other hand. She was dressed like Betty, in a collared white cotton shirt, brown dungarees, and tall boots, but her clothes were clean and dry and more finely made.

Pretty as a picture, Blanche Devens was, with fine features, smooth pale skin, and cupid's bow lips. Her red hair, the color of dried blood itself, swallowed the dim light of the cabin. Her pale blue eyes, the blue of the lightning flames, glowed.

Excitement? Pleasure?

Betty didn't know and didn't care.

Evie's daddy, John, sat on the far side of the dining room table, both hands flat on its rough surface like they were glued there. He was a quietly handsome dark-haired man some ten years older than Betty, with a sweet smile when he wasn't being tortured.

He was missing his right pinkie finger, blood pooling around the cauterized stump and soaking into the oak table.

Betty tried to keep her magic clean, channeling power through song.

Others stole life energy from other folks, through blood and fear and torture.

The room was warm, overly warm; a blaze roared in the field rock fireplace. Sugar maple logs.

"I'm taking the girl," Blanche said. She tossed John's finger into the fire, which flared up and devoured it. John slumped, knocking his head on the table, like the flames had sucked energy out of him, not just consumed his flesh.

"I won't let you do," Betty said.

Blanche blinked those pansy blue eyes at her. "Betty, you know I just can't live like this anymore. I need the city. I need culture. I need a way to get back."

"Blanche, you are a selfish piece of work." And a surprisingly sneaky witch. Betty had had no idea that Blanche had powers. Maybe that was how she hooked that businessman.

Not strong enough to keep him, though.

"One hick mountain girl and her daddy don't matter one bit."

Evie's fox cub darted around Betty and launched himself, growling, at Blanche. She laughed, a sweet musical laugh, and swept her hand in front of her. The fox cub smashed into the wall next to the fireplace. He didn't move. Evie cried out from behind Betty.

That forlorn gasp broke Betty's heart. She stepped aside. Evie rushed to the little fox and cradled him up.

Stepped aside—and nearer to the fireplace, where the flames were glowing more green than blue, now.

The green of Evie's eyes. Or the green of her momma Rose's.

John stirred, looked up blearily. He met Betty's eyes, glanced to the fireplace, then back to Betty. One small nod.

Clever man.

"See, that's the difference between you and me," Betty said. "Everyone matters to me."

Blanche tossed her head. "And that's why you're a scrawny spinster in dirty clothes, despite your power." She thrust both hands out, shoving Betty back against the wall with all the strength of the monsoon, knocking off her hat and cracking her skull against the thick logs.

Strong. So strong. And oh, did it hurt. Betty closed her eyes, felt herself slipping down the wall to the floor. She could feel her own power leaching out of her, captured by Blanche.

Jessie screamed, the shrill cry of a stallion facing a foe. The cry was so alien from her sweet horse it jarred Betty back to herself.

Betty croaked, *"I burst the bars asunder and set the prisoner free."* Her belly cramped and she gasped, retching, but John was standing, his eyes bright with pain and focus.

More than standing: he tackled Blanche and knocked her to the floor, next to the fireplace.

"And then the flames caught on her hair," Betty sang, clenching her fists, trying to stay upright. *"The lovely witch from Mayberryfaire."*

The bright green maple log flames leapt to Blanche as if all they'd wanted was permission.

"Let her up, John," Betty said.

Blanche screamed, swatting at her head, but her long curls blazed brighter, bright as fresh blood. The acrid smell of burning hair watered Betty's eyes.

Blanche's shirt caught fire next, and she staggered out the front door, keening.

Betty didn't think the rain could put out the fire. Not a fire fueled by Evie's daddy's love and her momma's protection, bound up in the sugar maple tree.

She kneeled next to Evie, still hugging her fox. *"And true love's kiss healed his mortal wounds,"* she crooned, nodding to Evie, who kissed the fox's head. The little fox squirmed to be set down, then ran out the front door, yipping.

They all followed the fox outside, John helping keep Betty steady on her feet.

The rain had let up, and the clouds were blowing out. Betty could see Venus glowing near the western horizon. A sprinkling of stars followed. The air smelled damp and cool, a breeze meandering over the hill.

A charred corpse lay in the mud, twenty feet from the cabin.

Blanche.

Jessie switched his thin tail against his flanks and stomped one hoof. Betty soothed him, stroking his soft muzzle, holding on to his neck more desperately than she wished she had to. Wobbly as a newborn colt, she was.

Betty reached up and patted the back of her head. Damp. Blood stained her fingers.

"I can try," Evie said, then repeated Betty's lyric, "*And true love's kiss healed his—her?—mortal wounds.*" Jessie obligingly licked Betty's face and snuffled in her hair, picking out hairpins with his sensitive lips til her hair fell in a tangle of curls down her back.

"Did it work?" Evie asked.

The wound itched. Betty could feel the skin knitting together, the swelling going down. "It's working," she said. She looked past Evie to Blanche's corpse and sucked in her breath.

A dainty copperhead snake wound itself around Blanche's thin blackened neck. It hissed at them.

Jessie trembled. He hated snakes, like any sensible horse.

But every creature of the woods has its purpose.

John went back into the cabin and returned, bearing a branch, green flames flickering from one end.

"Wait!" Betty said, watching the little snake.

"Go on your way, you are now free

"Go on your way, don't worry me—" Betty sang.

If snakes had eyebrows one would be arched.

Then it slithered away down the hill.

At Betty's nod, John walked to Blanche's corpse, then lowered the branch to the body.

The corpse flared and disintegrated, ash mixing with the mud.

"Better this way," he said. "No body, no questions." He'd wrapped a handkerchief around his wounded hand. "I'm going to brew some tea. With whiskey. Care to have some, Betty?"

———

A HALF HOUR LATER, Jessie was bedded down next to Blanche's warmblood mare in John's ramshackle barn, enjoying a meal of sweet feed and hay. Betty was dry and wearing one of Rose's old dresses, enjoying herself a cup of tea, with a generous shot of whiskey and a tablespoon of honey mixed in.

Evie sat next to her, her fox curled up on her feet.

"This is a scrapbook I made you," Betty said, flipping through the pages. "History to learn. Lessons for you to practice. Maybe you'll be a singer, like me. Maybe not."

"I want to be a singer," Evie said.

"Maybe you could manipulate the weather and winds, like Blanche."

"I don't want to be anything like her."

Betty nodded. "And that's why I'm going to help you."

John came in from the kitchen, carrying a big pot full of rabbit stew and three smaller bowls. "Getting it all worked out?" He kissed the top of Evie's head, then sat across from the two of them, ladling out stew.

"How'd you know to burn those logs, John?" asked Betty.

He stared at the fireplace. "I couldn't save Rose," he said finally. "But I always felt she was still around, somehow. Still around to take care of her baby girl.

"When Evie found Kit, I knew she was in danger. So I chopped down the maple tree and always kept a log or two burning. Just felt right. Just wish I could have done more."

"I think, when Blanche tossed that finger of yours into the fire, she created a link. I think that's what gave Rose the strength to destroy her; the strength she took from you. I couldn't have done a thing more than I did," Betty said, touching his hand.

"Can you stay a night or two?" John asked, then turned beet red. "I mean, to start teaching Evie?"

"Course I can," Betty said, eyeing him. He did have that sweet smile. "More than happy to stay on for a bit."

And maybe it was time to have a man. At least for a bit.

VICTORY GIRL

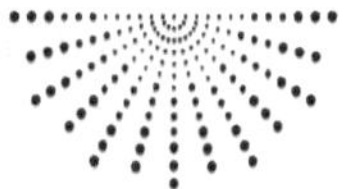

R uthie dug her fingers into the rich moist earth, gently tugging on the root ball of the dandelion, not caring if she got dirt under her nails. A fat earthworm came up with the dandelion, wriggling in the bright early morning sunshine. She shook the clump of roots and dirt gently, freeing up the worm. It dove quick and deep into the earth.

A quick puttering roar announced a test flight. Ruthie leaned back on her heels, heart stuttering in time as she watched the fuselage-free test plane swoop overhead. Just a skeleton of a plane, really. Easier to tweak things that way. She watched til it became a tiny speck, flying back north to Los Angeles. What she wouldn't give....

Breathing in the tang of the tomato leaves, heating in the warm sun, Ruthie plucked off dandelion leaves to save them for salad tonight. *Focus, girl.* The rest would go into the scrap pile to feed the garden and the chickens. Waste not, want not.

The dark red cherry tomatoes were ripe already, and she popped one in her mouth, enjoying the hot sweetness as it burst all juicy. Just one, all the more special for the indulgence. She wiped sweat off her forehead and dug up another dandelion.

Garden Grove was well named. Her mama's Victory Garden

"

thrived, especially now Ruthie was done with school for the summer and could tend it. Now, in mid July, it was producing a bounty that would feed the two of them as well as several of their neighbors.

Ruthie didn't know if she'd go back to school in the fall. She was sixteen, and she could get a job in the Douglas Aircraft Plant down in Long Beach just as easily as her mama. She was good with her hands. Clever with mechanical things. Even if she didn't get to fly herself, she could help others fly. The war effort required every bit a patriot could give. School was a waste, compared to beating Hitler and the Japanese.

Her mama would be home soon. She worked the night shift along with Mrs. Flores from down the street and Ms Kitchener next door, and the three of them borrowed old Mr. Robbin's rust and blue Ford truck Mildred to get there and back.

Mrs. Flores' husband was an infantry man overseas in Italy, and Ms Kitchener never married, and Ruthie's pa died in the earthquake of '33 when Ruthie was just a little girl, so all the ladies were coming home to empty beds.

Ruthie asked her mama once if she weren't lonely.

"Men!" Rosalie Isley said, her blue eyes sparking and her cheeks flushed red as her long curly hair. An Irish rose, straight from the old country. "More trouble than they're worth, girl. And you don't want to get a reputation as a Victory Girl, chasing after men, claiming it's your patriotic duty. Those sailors are the worst. Don't you forget that. Worse than a pack of love talkers, lurking to ensnare a young woman and suck the life out of her."

"I was just asking about you, mama. Don't worry about me." Ruthie thought her mama was too pretty to give up on men so easily. And too superstitious. Love talkers? No such thing. Not in today's world of steel and engines.

And there was no chance Ruthie was going to make a fool of herself over some boy. But there was no changing her mama's mind once it was set on something.

And Ruthie didn't *quite* agree with her mama. Oh, Bobby Kincaid who tugged her braids back in sixth grade was a rat, and even if he had offered her a handful of ripe boysenberries the day before school let out, she wouldn't give him the time of day. But Mrs. Flores' husband's nephew Frankie, with those dark brown eyes and lashes out to there...well, he was handsome. When he smiled at her, that sideways quirk of his upper lip, that dimple in his chin deepening.... He was taking her on a date this afternoon.

Two more rows and she'd be done weeding the garden.

Maybe she could borrow Mr. Robbins' truck Mildred and she and Frankie could drive down to the Pike in Long Beach. The Cyclone Racer coaster was still running, and it was bound to be cooler on the ocean that here in Garden Grove. She'd ridden the big wooden coaster only once, and the rushing descent sparked more butterflies in her stomach than even Frankie's smile. It had to be like flying a plane, even if just a little bit.

The purr of an engine and gravel crunching under tires broke into her thoughts.

"Ain't you a pretty sight," a soft lilting voice said.

Ruthie glanced up, squinting.

A man stood in front of her, with eyes bluer than Sinatra's, smooth alabaster skin that had never been kissed by the sun, and midnight gleaming hair glossier than his fine leather boots. He wore a black wool suit with creases in the pants sharper than his cheekbones, and a crisp white shirt that looked dingy compared to his skin. A thin black leather tie, with a turquoise big as an egg tucked up against the man's throat, dangled halfway down his broad chest.

He held a carved wooden pipe in one hand, smoke lazing out of it to tickle her nose with tobacco and spearmint and a scent she couldn't figure out, and a black fedora in the other hand.

Behind him...was that a 1938 Cadillac V-16? Just the fastest accelerating car in the world. She longed to touch it, let alone drive it.

"I'm all dirty and sweaty and I have no idea what you're talking about," Ruthie said, her stomach clenching.

Her mama Rosalie was drop dead gorgeous, all soft curves and thick dark red hair tamed into smooth Victory rolls.

No one ever commented on Ruthie's looks.

No, not Ruthie, with her frizzy strawberry blond hair, sharp featured freckled face, and stubby nails always grubby with grease. Not Ruthie, wearing her mama's cast off, too-tight work shirt, stretching across her breasts in front and her muscled shoulders in back.

"Beauty's in the eye of the beholder," the man said, taking a puff on his pipe, his smooth lips wrapping around the stem. Ruthie couldn't look away. "How 'bout I take you out for a vanilla coke, or an ice cream sundae? Whipped cream, sprinkles of nuts, and a cherry on top?"

"I'm busy, mister," she said, clenching her fists. Her eyes kept skating from the man, to his car. Oh Lord, that car! It outshined the man. Candy apple red hood and fenders against a gleaming gold body, white walled tires without a speck of dust to mar them, chrome spokes reflecting the sky like mirrors. Red canvas top tucked down.

Frankie. Think of Frankie with his sweet smile.

"Come on, baby doll. Maybe later? Take you for a ride in my car? Looks like you have a good eye for a fine machine."

"I'm busy later, too," Ruthie said, yearning belying her words.

"Fair enough," he said, puffing once more on his pipe. The wood glowed gold in the sunlight. "Maybe I'll get lucky later." He smiled, a slow sweet smile, put his hat on, nodded, and drove off.

———

RUTHIE BROUGHT Mr. Robbins a basket of sweet tomatoes and a couple alligator pears and two small hard limes. His dark seamed face lit up.

"Ah, Ruthie, you didn't have to. But thank you kindly. And don't you look pretty?"

Ruthie looked down sheepishly. She'd cleaned up and changed into her one good blouse that she hadn't yet outgrown, white with ruffles along the v neckline, and a cream colored skirt with little pink flowers, that she'd sewn at school. Her hair was smoothed down and pinned back with a green Bakelite barrette shaped like a bow.

"Now, just bring Mildred back in time for your mama tonight. And if you could take a look at her darn ignition switch in the next day or two, I'd greatly appreciate it. You okay if she quits on you?"

Ruthie had hand cranked the old truck more times than she could remember. "I'm fine, Mr. Robbins. You know I'm strong. I can spend all day tomorrow going over her if you'd like." Her thoughts drifted to the red and gold Cadillac coupe. She'd love to get her hands on it, that was for sure.

"You're a sweet girl, Ruthie. Have a nice time with Frankie," he added, smiling. "Tell him, he doesn't treat you right, I'll bust his chops."

"I—" Ruth started, then laughed. "I will, Mr. Robbins."

———

Sure enough, she had to crank the engine to get Mildred going. Tomorrow she'd fix her. Tomorrow. She was flushed and awkward by the time the motor was chuckling along.

But then Frankie let her drive the both of them all the way to the Pike. That was even better than his dimples or long eyelashes, though he looked nice in his pressed chinos and plaid shirt, setting off his dark skin. He was small and lanky, and had a lot of growing to do, to fill out his boy's frame, but her mama had said, over tea with Mrs. Flores one afternoon, that he certainly had potential.

Then they'd both giggled. Hmph.

Ruthie felt huge and ungainly next to him.

She gunned Mildred down the back roads, Frankie squeezing the dash so hard his knuckles were white.

She was trying her darnedest to not think about the Cadillac. The purr of its engine.

Or its driver, Mr. Cadillac, with those piercing, knowing blue eyes. *Ain't you a pretty sight.*

The Cyclone Racer jutted hundreds of feet out over the beach on the long pier, thick pilings sunk into what used to be the ocean floor until the sandy beach grew to fill it in. The wooden track supports were so dense Ruthie couldn't see the breakwater on the other side of the pier. She didn't know how the coaster hadn't just sank into the sand, and been swallowed by the ocean, it was so massive, rather than reaching for the clouds.

It smelled like brine and grease and taffy and popcorn and sweat, all mingled together in a glorious heady mess.

"It's got two tracks, Frankie, so the cars can race each other, and it can go over fifty miles an hour. I felt like I was flying, coming down the tallest hill. And then it finishes with these little hills, so little they seem silly, but with each one, it feels like you just fly, higher and higher." Ruthie tugged on his hand, hurrying him along through the small crowds of sailors and high school kids, past the tattoo parlors and palm readers' shops and the salt water taffy stands with their red and white striped awnings.

Even in the mid afternoon the crowd was building. She stood up on tippy toes, peering towards the Cyclone Racer. There wasn't much of a line yet, that she could see.

A man wearing black hat tugged low, with a turquoise stone at his throat, stood at the counter of the ice cream shop kitty corner to them. Mr. Cadillac. How did he get here? Surely she would've seen his car.

He licked the top of the scoop of ice cream, and her cheeks flushed. *Beauty's in the eye of the beholder.*

She scooched closer to Frankie.

"Is it safe?" Frankie asked. "I heard some kid fell out and died."

"Only because they were dumb," Ruthie said. "And that was the Hi Boy coaster in Venice, anyhow." She nodded towards the Hippodrome and its painted horses. Past Mr. Cadillac. Who she just wouldn't stare at. "There's a carousel. Is that more your speed? Would you rather ride that?"

"Come on, baby doll," Frankie said, frowning.

Come on, baby doll. Ruthie dropped his hand. "Well, I'm riding the Cyclone. If you want to join me, I'd be happy to ride it with you. But you're not spoiling my fun."

"I didn't say I wouldn't ride it," he said.

She quickened her steps. Maybe she wasn't as pretty as her mama. But she was strong and fast and brave. And she wanted to ride that darn coaster, throw her arms up in the air, and, just for a moment, feel like she was flying.

———

THE LINE WAS short for the coaster. Before she knew, she was seated in the front seat of the first car, left side, with Frankie to her right, gripping the safely bar like his life depended on it.

The train trundled forward into a dark tunnel, then out. She blinked in the sunlight as they started clanking up the first hill.

At the top of that hill, their track met up with the opposing train's track. She didn't have any way to control what train went faster 'round the track, but she wanted to see her opponents, nonetheless.

Mr. Cadillac smiled at her, teeth gleaming in the late afternoon sun. He was holding his hat, she supposed in his lap, against those crisply pressed wool trousers, and the ocean breeze tossed his hair. His cheeks were flushed a soft pink. He was by himself in the front seat, first car, but was pressed against the right side of the car, like he was trying his damnedest to get up against her.

"Let's go for a ride, baby," he said softly, his words tickling against her throat like he sat only a few inches from her, not five feet.

Ruthie stared straight ahead. She wouldn't look, she wouldn't, she would ignore him and he would just go away. Frankie gripped her right hand just as the car barreled downhill. She yanked her hand away.

Mr. Cadillac's train had edged past hers on the downhill, but hers passed his as they ascended the next hill and entered the quick banked turn to the next downhill.

The trains kept swapping positions until the last stretch, the series of quick rollers.

"Go, go, go!" Ruthie screamed, flinging her arms in the air. With each dip, she rose a little bit, the safety bar shifting, til on the last she felt five feet, ten, twenty above the car, hands reaching for the clouds.

She couldn't help it, she looked to the left.

Mr. Cadillac was there, right next to her, up in the air, eyes burning, a hectic flush across those sharp cheekbones. Close enough she could smell the spearmint and tobacco and something else.

Close enough to touch those soft lips.

"Fly with me," he whispered, holding out his hand.

She reached to him.

Someone behind her screamed, and Ruthie turned to her right (don't look to her left, *don't* look at Mr. Cadillac again), even though, as they pulled back into the loading station, the tracks had already split, and she wouldn't be able to see him, even if she wanted.

And Ruthie didn't *want*. She didn't.

Frankie slumped against the side of the car, eyes closed, blood pouring from a gash on his forehead.

"Oh no, no, what happened—" She touched his face, Frankie's sweet face, his throat. She could feel a pulse, strong and steady.

"That last bump," the woman behind them sobbed. "He just rose up and smacked his head along the overhead beam."

"Open your eyes, baby, open them," Ruthie begged as she stroked his hair. The train slowed to a stop. "I need a doctor!"

"Ruthie?" Frankie murmured. He slowly opened his eyes, squinted. "Ruthie, what happened?"

The attendant helped her lift him out. Frankie was looking around, eyes blinking slowing. "I need to sit down, Ruthie."

Mr. Cadillac was gone.

———

OF COURSE there wasn't a doctor. But a young nurse on shore leave, still dressed in her trim black uniform with her brunette hair pinned up, took one look at the blood clotting on Frankie's face and took charge, directing Frankie to a wooden bench and pestering the attendant for a rag and some fresh water.

"You go get yourself a coke and some taffy," she said to Ruthie, her voice soft and twanging. She pressed two quarters into Ruthie's sweaty palm. "And bring back a coke for your friend, here. He'll be fine."

"I—" Ruthie stumbled. This was her fault, all her fault, she'd made him ride the Cyclone when he didn't want to—

"Git. I don't want to take care of more than one patient, right now. You need something to occupy all those thoughts in your head." The nurse shooed her away. "Git."

Ruthie trudged away, her feet, her body, solidly attached to the ground. Ice cream. She'd get herself a cone, and Frankie a root beer float with cherry syrup. He loved those. Too sweet for her, but he loved them.

"Hey, baby doll."

She didn't need to look up. She'd known he'd be waiting for her. Mr. Cadillac, with his lilting voice and blue, blue eyes. That sharp pink tongue darting out to lick his ice cream cone. Or to lick his smooth lips. That spearmint and tobacco scent, heavy against her face.

The sun was setting, and she knew, even as it inched closer to the horizon, that once its green flash was gone, and the fairway lit up, she…she didn't know if she could say no.

The Victory Girls would be out, looking for sailors to comfort.

She wasn't any better than them. Maybe worse. *Definitely* worse.

Why was Mr. Cadillac not in uniform? He was mid twenties, maybe a little older. A full grown man. Hale enough to be serving in the Navy or Army, with that broad chest and those strong hands. Those sharp eyes that saw everything, everything that she wanted. He didn't need or deserve any comfort from her.

She'd be one of those loose girls her mama warned her about.

"Baby doll, it's okay. He's not right for you. You need to fly, baby doll. He'll just hold you down." He took her hands. His were icy, freezing, and she looked up.

"I'll let you drive the Cadillac. Take me out for a ride," he said. His lips quirked. "A test flight."

There was nothing else except him. The sounds of the sailors, the women and the kids let loose for the summer, tearing some time away from their jobs and the war, all of it faded. The smell of the popcorn and taffy blew out with the ocean breeze. Even that tapered. The sun had set and the lights were sparking on, but nothing was as bright as his blue eyes.

All of it faded.

Til it was just him, Mr. Cadillac, and her.

He leaned in, burying his face in her hair. "You smell so good, baby doll. Sunlight and growing things." He breathed softly against her neck, behind her ears, and pulled one of her hands behind her back, pressing her against him.

Why had she thought he was cold? He was burning up against her.

She moaned, a sound she'd never made before. He was strong, stronger than her. Taller. Bigger. She felt small. Felt like she should just give in. Surrender.

"Say yes, baby doll. Let's get out of here. Just say yes." He lowered his lips to hers.

If he hadn't been holding her up, she'd be flat on the ground, with the bubble gum wrappers and cigarette butts and sand. She'd never felt anything like this, anything, her belly and thighs heavy, and between—

"No." She could hardly hear herself. But she said it.

"No?" He pulled back. "Baby doll, you know you want to say yes. You have to say yes."

"No. No, I don't." She yanked her hands from his and stumbled back. "I'm better than this. If I say yes, it's because *I* want to. Not because some sweet talking man with a fast car who I don't even know tries to—to seduce me."

She kept walking backwards, bumping into people, but no one noticed her. No one saw her.

No one except him.

Buildings were coming back into focus, the Hippodrome with its painted ponies closest to her.

"Little girl, I haven't even *started* trying."

The bass thrums of the pipe organ from the Hippodrome sounded far, far away even as it segued into a bright tinkling song. She turned to look at the carousel, the brightness of the lights causing her to squint and tear up.

The horses circled, their motion like waves on the shore, endless, repetitive.

"I can work with that," he said, reaching around her waist. He pressed against her in time with the horses, maintaining their rhythm even as her vision clouded again, as she sighed and leaned back against him. He reached one hand up under her skirt, stroking her thigh. The other cupped her breast.

She could give in.

She could.

But she wouldn't.

He was holding her against the side of the wooden building that housed the carousel.

"You smell so good," Ruthie said, and it wasn't even a lie. She could breathe him in forever. "Is it your pipe?"

She could feel his smirk, even if she couldn't see it. Feel it in how he gripped her.

"Want to suck on it?" he asked, voice teasing. Confident.

"Can I taste it?"

He stopped exploring under her skirt. She felt his hand move back, between them, but into his pocket.

"Light it?" she asked. "Or just let me?"

He passed her the pipe and a small lighter, engraved with tiny flowers. "You know how?"

"I know a lot more than you think I do," she said, lighting the pipe and breathing in. Tobacco and mint, and something else, something that was all him, heady and thick. *Lovetalker*. "Let's go back here. Far side the carousel. Unless we can take a ride?"

"Of course, baby doll," he said, voice brightening. "Anything you want. Just jump on when I tell you—now!"

She jumped on the rotating platform, dodging around the bejeweled, white horses in their ceaseless circular leaps, past the riders who seemed to not see her, or Mr. Cadillac. She held his pipe in one hand, and the lighter in the other.

"Hold me?" she asked.

"Yes, my love, yes—" he said, blue eyes shining like hungry stars. He wrapped his arms around her.

He smelled so, so good. Felt so right. He was kissing her, tongue thrusting into her mouth, and her head spun.

But she kept back a small part of herself.

She lit the lighter and tossed it towards the center wooden construct of the carousel, containing the motor, the central pole, and all the gearing. She followed it with the pipe.

The flames were tiny, tentative, even, at first, licking along the base, brightening as they devoured the wood with its gilt paint. Then, with a roar, the center caught. Whether it was grease from the bearings, or just the wood, dried and cured in the ocean breeze over the years, she didn't know.

She heard screams as the riders scrambled for safety, even as she closed her eyes and twined her tongue around his. Just once.

Then she pulled back.

"The answer is no. I can learn to fly on my own."

She jumped off the platform and headed back to the Cyclone Racer, straightening her blouse and skirt as she ran.

Ignoring the wail of anguish behind her, as the carousel burned.

———

SHE DIDN'T SEE the Cadillac when she got herself and Frankie to Mr. Robbin's truck Mildred. She didn't know if that made her sad or if it made her happy.

Or just tired.

Sure 'nough, the starter acted up. She sighed.

She drove sedately back to Garden Grove, swinging by Frankie's mom's house, a small Craftsman bungalow that had survived the earthquake of '33.

"Are you going to be okay?" she asked, stroking Frankie's face. She got out of the truck and circled to the passenger side, helping him climb out. He was a bit unsteady, still, though that kind nurse said he should be fine, before the nurse ran to see if anyone was hurt in the fire.

Lucky, with a hard head, but he should be fine.

"I think so," he said, voice soft, brown eyes confused. "I don't really remember what happened."

"Well, let's just say I won't be taking you on anymore roller coasters," she teased, then sobered. "I'm sorry, Frankie. Sorry I made you."

"It's okay," he said.

She leaned forward and kissed him. Softly, then more firmly as he hugged her to him, as he returned the kiss with interest.

"You can take me on a roller coaster any day if that's what happens afterwards," he said.

"I'll come check on you tomorrow, okay, Frankie?" she said. "Sleep well. I gotta get Mildred back to my mom before she needs to go on her shift."

He nodded.

She watched Frankie until he was safely inside, then walked back to the driver's side.

Against which leaned Mr. Cadillac.

"You owe me a pipe, baby doll," Mr. Cadillac said, his voice rough. He had soot on his cheekbones and ash in his glossy hair. The turquoise at his throat was cracked, and the pleats in his pants all limp. His eyes were banked fire.

"I don't owe you a damn thing," Ruthie said. She shoved past him to climb into the truck, not feeling the slightest warmth in her belly, not feeling the tiniest bit of desire. She put the truck into gear and pressed the ignition button. *Don't act up now*, she begged Mildred. *Don't act up now. I promise, I'll fix you tomorrow.*

The engine sputtered to life. Mr Cadillac scrambled out of the way.

Ruthie drove home, wishing she couldn't still smell spearmint and tobacco. Hoping someday, she'd forget how damn good he had smelled, even all tattered and ragged.

But she was free. She knew it in her heart.

She was free to fly.

THE SONGS OF THEIR LIVES

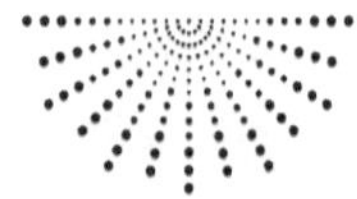

"You cain't sing your normal songs. I heard what you done put in them, the ideas you put in folks' heads, and you cain't sing them here." Tommy Joe, the owner of J.D.'s Bar, rocked back on the heels of his scuffed steel-toed work boots. His belly, encased by a tight red t-shirt with the bar's logo (two cans of cheap-ass beer, with little stick arms and legs, dancing together), hung over his tarnished rodeo belt buckle. His knuckles were scarred and green with old bruises.

Tommy Joe stretched past his six-foot height, puffing out his chest. He already had nearly a foot on Darla Jean, with her just five foot two.

Some men just needed *more*.

Darla, perched on a rickety wooden stool, fixing to tune her guitar, looked up at Tommy Joe. She clenched her white plastic guitar pick between her teeth as she pulled her curly red hair back into a ponytail. Tommy Joe's doughy face was screwed up, maybe with distaste, maybe regret, but it didn't matter none.

The guitar pick snapped, and she tasted sweet coppery blood, marveling at the rich taste. The solid human taste.

It wasn't sweet enough to cover up the smell of stale beer assaulting her nose. Or the rank body odor of Tommy Joe, standing way too close.

The flip side of being able to smell coffee and whiskey and hot fresh donuts. You had to deal with the stink of the living.

She spat out the pieces of the pick and Tommy Joe jerked back two steps, chest deflating.

"I can come up with a playlist suited to your bar," Darla said. "Don't you worry none."

There was magic in her songs, real magic, the magic to grant wishes. To give a person a second chance. Sometimes it granted invisibility, just enough for a woman to sneak out of a situation, when her man never left her unobserved. Sometimes a worn leather purse appeared that always had coin, leastwise for a month or two. Sometimes healing and health, enough so a broken woman could walk away on her own.

And sometimes, it just showed there was another way, if you had the courage to reach for it.

No goddam way she was going to let Tommy Joe bully her.

No one ever got to bully Darla Jean anymore.

She focused on her acoustic guitar, the warm golden wood gleaming in the dim light. She plucked the thickest string, then twisted the tuning peg til the guitar thrummed a low E. The sound echoed off the cigarette-smoke varnished black walls of the room, off the sticky dark brown linoleum floor tiles.

Darla worked her way through the rest of the strings, taking in the rest of the bar while she did. She was perched up on the ten by six foot stage, set opposite the long wooden bar with its host of red vinyl barstools. She couldn't see herself in the long mirror stretching behind it, the mirror was so fogged with dust and grime. The stoic black eyes of a dead buck, head mounted to the left of the mirror, met hers.

Run away, the buck whispered. *Run away, or you'll end up just like me. You cain't play your way out of everything.*

I'm not like you, anchored to one spot. I'm free. I can go anywhere, she whispered back. *Anywhere I'm needed.*

Country band stickers plastered the black walls and ceiling next to the bar. Some old campaign stickers, too, ranging from Duke for President '88 (and boy did she remember living through *that* nonsense, with that white-sheeted bigot) to more recent bumper stickers bearing anti-Obama slogans and crowing about MAGA.

Figured.

Cheap bottles of likely watered-down liquor filled a small shelf under the mirror. Most folks probably just drank beer. Looked like J.D.'s had both kinds of beer...regular *and* light. Probably watered down too.

Tommy Joe left around the D string for the back office, banging his leg on one of the rickety wooden chairs clustered around equally rickety stained tables, muttering to himself about uppity broads.

Darla couldn't bring herself to care about his masculine sensitivities.

She had a life to save.

———

J.D.'s didn't have any sort of dressing room, and by the time Darla was due to get ready for her set, the ladies' already had a line five women deep.

Tommy Joe directed her to a tiny storage room. The room smelled of stale sex and rat droppings. Guess it was used for more than storage, despite the cases of industrial toilet paper and beer kegs stacked on pallets filling most the floor.

The lock was busted, too. She leaned back against the door to keep it closed as she changed. Wondered how many women had gotten splinters in their ass from the old door.

She shimmied into her show gear, thirty years old but still fashionable: black leather pants tight over her thighs, bootcut legs loose around her calves; a deep vee royal-blue sequined tank top with just a few sequins missing; and a cropped fringed black leather jacket, the shine just a bit dulled.

Darla didn't have any shoes besides her black alligator cowboy boots, but they fit the outfit just fine. She tugged them on, pulling the legs of her leathers over top of the boots rather than tucking them in.

She folded up her jeans, the knees worn through with age, not fashion, and stuffed them into her guitar case. She added her faded black cotton bra, panties, and ribbed black tank. She wore a wispy lace thong and a black satin push up bra under her stage clothes. Sexy, but just for her. Not for anyone else.

Nearly ready.

A warrior readying for a battle, though nobody but her knew it. She put her turquoise cuff on her left wrist, and the snowflake obsidian cuff on her right. Turquoise for protection. Obsidian for perseverance and strength.

Oh, hell, they were just pretty. Hadn't really helped her *before*, had they?

She freed her red curls from the ponytail, running her fingers through it, fluffing it out. Her makeup was sparse: a bit of tinted moisturizer for her face, charcoal eye shadow for that smoky look around her ice blue eyes, and black mascara to thicken her lashes. That was it. That was enough.

"You ready, girl?" Tommy Joe barked from outside. "Don't you forget what I done told you."

Darla had to wonder. Was it Tommy Joe's woman, that would hear Darla's song? And, Lord willing, act upon it? Or someone else?

Didn't matter, as long as the one she was called to save heard and acted.

She pushed her way to the tiny stage, protecting her guitar from errant elbows, trying not to breathe in the miasma of cheap cologne and sweat. J.D.'s was packed to the gills, men bellowing to be heard over their neighbors. Darla didn't have any illusion that the crowd was for her. Far as Tommy Joe was concerned, someone like Darla —*especially* like Darla, with her kitten sweet face and tight little body —was just eye candy for his patrons. Not somebody to take seriously.

Though maybe someone did. Someone who gave Tommy Joe a heads-up about her songs.

Darla seated herself on her stool. Got as comfy as she could. It was just her and her guitar. Well, and the clear plastic beer pitcher she'd snagged as a tip jar, seeding it with a five and a couple ones to give people the idea.

The red bulbs of the stage lights painted her face bloody and turned her blue sequined top violet. She hated red stage lights.

She strummed, checking her tuning, then began playing. Her rich voice, deep for her size, started off soft, soft enough folks had to quiet down to hear her.

And they did, drawn to the petite redhead with her big husky voice, singing the songs of their lives.

She sang old songs, songs of injustice and loss and hard work with no end in sight, her guitar moaning along with her. Sang long enough to need a drink of water and to want a shot of whiskey, both of which someone was kind enough to set in front of her.

And then she started sing the old murder ballads. The songs that would've brought her fame, back when, if not for a vindictive brute of a manager.

Women killed for their man's convenience. Killed for an unwanted baby. Killed for an unwelcome love. Or killed because the man felt it was just time to move on.

Shot, drowned, gutted. *Pearl Bryan, Omie Wise. Darla Jean.* Even old *Tom Dooley*, about poor Laurie Foster, with her name erased by his even in death.

Darla *stretched*, feeling the reactions of the folks in the audience as she played.

That woman, *there*. The pretty blonde with her hair blown out shiny straight, her makeup thick but precise. Her tight hot pink t-shirt hid the bruises on her belly. Darla could feel the echo of fists against her own gut. But she could also feel the determination of the blonde. She'd be leaving soon, never to return. Maybe pushed by Darla's songs, maybe not.

The blonde didn't need Darla. She wasn't the reason Darla was here.

That skinny brunette, with her sad brown eyes?

The brunette wouldn't leave, no matter what; Darla's gift could tell. If Darla dragged her off, the brunette would run back to her man lickety split. The brunette had done it twice before, suffering worse each time she returned to her man. Do it again and she'd be dead. Sooner rather than later, though later was a given.

Some things magic just couldn't fix.

But who? Who was it, who needed her help so much Darla was pulled a hundred miles out off her normal route? She finished the last of the murder ballads she regularly sang. Took a sip of water from the glass that someone had kindly refilled. Drank the shot of whiskey that had replaced the first, soothing the rawness in her throat.

"I hope ya'll are enjoying the music," Darla said. "I'd like to play something special for you, now. Something I came up with on my own."

Tommy Joe, behind the bar, tensed.

Darla picked a jaunty tune on her guitar, the music a counterpart to the simple lyrics she'd penned.

You know what he's gonna do
You think it's what you deserve
But I'm here to tell you
There's a justice I can serve
It's not running away
If there's something to run to
So live another day
Girl, you have to know that's true

The blonde tossed back her drink and left. The skinny brunette, staring at the floor, tucked herself next to the beefy man that must be her husband.

And a slender young man dressed in tight jeans and a stained white t-shirt met Darla's eyes square on.

Help me. His thick black lashes fluttered over bittersweet chocolate brown eyes. Pain. So much pain, pulsing off his slender body.

"Time for me to take a break, folks. Thanks for the whiskey, but don't forget my tip jar here." She nudged the pitcher with one booted toe. "That's the gas money to get me out of here, 'cause ya'll don't want to hear all these songs more'n once, and I'm near the end of my reper-toire. Back in a few, folks."

———

DARLA ALWAYS LEFT the cash in the tip jar. Taking it would cue someone she wasn't coming back on stage.

She headed straight for the storage room. She wouldn't have the time to change, but she'd grab her guitar case and get her guitar packed up safely.

The young man had threaded the crowd after her.

What would the magic grant him?

It wasn't the first time she'd helped a man. It was just rare.

"Who you runnin' from, kid?" Darla asked as she packed up her guitar. She bet she'd had a solid ten years on the kid. He couldn't be older than twenty-two or -three. He had those chocolate brown eyes, dark against his tanned skin, despite the bruise ringing the left eye. Cheekbones to die for. Maybe with her aid, he wouldn't. Barely as tall as her five foot two, but with smooth gym muscles. Long silky dark hair pulled back and up in man bun.

Pretty.

"Tommy Joe," he whispered. "My boyfriend. I've heard about you. The singer that rescues battered women."

"I help whoever needs it. What's your name?"

"Jayce," he said, voice a little stronger. Hopeful.

"Okay. My car's out back. The blue Gremlin."

"You're kidding."

"It runs—" *on magic and duct tape, but he didn't need to know that* "—and come on, do you think anyone would steal it?"

Anyone who really knew cars actually might. It was a Gremlin XR with a V8 engine. Only twenty-five built. But she didn't tell anyone that. Or let anyone look under the hood. She'd bought it new from a dealer in Arizona in '72 with money saved up from a year of gigs.

"Come on, kid. Let's get going."

———

THE BACK PARKING lot was lined by weeds and filled with broken glass and gravel, with a few spots delineated by broken concrete-and-rebar parking blocks. Her Gremlin and a white pickup she figured was Tommy Joe's were the only vehicles parked in back. The rutted weedy dirt driveway that led to the back lot kept the patrons up front.

An owl hooted and flew overhead on down silenced wings. Crickets chirped. Frogs cheeped.

And the skinny brunette stood up and leaned against the hood of the Gremlin.

"Can you help me?" she asked. "He thinks I'm in the bathroom. Your song—you're right. I don't deserve this. I can find a better life. I was in school to be a nurse when I met him. I can do that."

"Ma'am, I'm really sorry, but Darla ain't gonna be helping no one," Jayce said, stepping back from Darla and the Gremlin.

Tommy Joe exited the bar, a shotgun in his left hand, picking his way through the broken bits of glass and the cracked concrete parking blocks. Gave Jayce a hug and a peck on top of his head. "I warned you, Darla. If you'd just kept your mouth shut. You were fine up to the last song."

Darla stared at the shotgun. At Jayce. Then at the brunette. Save the one she could. "Are you sure, honey? Because it won't be easy. If you go back to him...."

"Don't ignore me, you stupid bitch."

"He'll kill me the next time. I know it. But he'll kill me for sure if I stay."

"Get in the car," Darla said. "Hide down in the back. I'll get you out of here."

Maybe Darla's gift, her gut, was wrong. Maybe the brunette *could* escape.

"You ain't going nowhere." Tommy Joe pumped the shotgun, Jayce tucked against his side.

"Jayce, honey, there's room for you, too," Darla said. "I can see what he's done to you. What he will do."

"He loves me. He said he'd never hit me again." Jayce kicked a piece of glass. It shattered against the concrete block.

Darla had heard that sad story too many times before.

Lived and died through it herself.

"I'm sorry, Jayce. Maybe the next time I come through," said Darla. "Tommy Joe, step aside, or I'll run you over and not even be a bit sorry."

He fired the shotgun, not ten feet away.

And missed, as Darla's form shimmered.

Pumped the shotgun again, fired again, missed again as Darla ghosted once more.

"Give up, Tommy Joe. You're just wasting ammo." She was solid as before, but her eyes, ice blue before, were dark as the star-studded sky.

"What the fuck are you?"

"Someone who didn't get out in time," Darla Jean said. "But who now has the power to help those who might just make it."

She opened the driver's door on the Gremlin, the hinges creaking like the dead come to life. "Jayce ain't ready yet. But he'll leave you one day. And I'll be here to help him.

"I'll always be here."

THE LIFE OF STUFFED TOYS

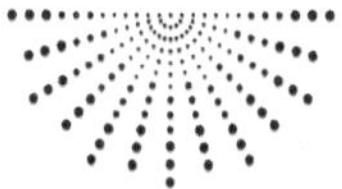

Three cats: one chocolate point Siamese, one marble brown tabby with white paws, one pitch black. Their eyes, imperious blue, warm honey, absinthe green, blazed at her, Southern California morning sunlight illuminating the intricate fused glass eyeballs set into their plush, realistic heads. Dust motes floated off their fake fur bodies, even though Lara fluffed them out weekly.

"You sure you want to bring them with you to college?" Lara's mom, Julie, asked. "Stuffed toys?" She placed an empty box by the foot of Lara's bed, an old-fashioned iron twin made up with quilts her Grandma DeeDee had handcrafted before she passed. Four other boxes full of jeans and blouses and sandals and sneakers were already taped up, ready to be packed into her mom's Subaru Forester.

There wasn't any replica of Grandma DeeDee, containing *her* ashes. Julie had an urn on the mantle for Grandma.

The cats sat on top of the bookcase next to her bed. Watching over her. Listening to music with her. Keeping her company while she worked on coding and homework, struggling to learn as much as she could, as quickly as she could. Something, some knowledge, always seemed just out of reach.

The cats encouraged her. Between their realistic little bodies, and her memories of each of them, they pushed her to learn.

Brulee, whose deep guttural squawks had belied his slender frame. He would twine his paws into her hair as they both slept, warm cocoa fur against her bright red hair, his cream body warm in her arms.

He passed when she was eight. Kidney failure. Mom sobbed harder than when Lara's dad left them, when Brulee died.

Pecan was just a kitten, brought in to the mellow the inevitable sorrow as Brulee aged, when they adopted her from a neighbor whose cat had a litter of four kittens. Pecan was feisty and playful and curious.

So curious, she slipped outside the front door when Lara's mom was signing for a package. Pecan came back that later that day, and the next, and the next, til one day she just didn't. They found her limp body the day after on the side of the road. Lara was twelve.

Abyss, Biss, a shy lanky teenager of a cat, lurked by the high school cafeteria trashcans, begging for scraps, until Lara brought him home last fall. He'd won her over with his sweet nature.

He had feline leukemia. Died just after last Christmas.

Lara had found a website that would make stuffed toy replicas of your pets from photos.

They did a good job, she thought when she opened the box in late February, just two months after she'd lost Biss. Especially with Pecan, catching the unique gold and chocolate whorls of her coat just so. Biss and Brulee were a bit more generic, young jet black tom and chocolate point Siamese, but they'd captured Biss's plushness and Brulee's sleekness.

They didn't smell like her cats, though. That dry scent that smelled nothing like their mouths, and weren't cats all just coated with cat spit?

A lavender and juniper sachet had been tucked in with the stuffed cats. That's what they smelled like. And over time, that soft piney scent brought her peace, just like the real cat smell.

Her mom had offered to get her another cat, after Lara had received the shipment from the replica company.

"We could go to the shelter over spring break," Julie had said, one gray day in March. "I miss having a cat, too."

"I have three cats," Lara said. "Three's enough."

Brulee and Pecan and Biss had all been cremated, their ashes returned in little canisters in blue velvet bags with golden cords. They'd ended up in the garage, tucked away with the broken crockpot and worn out Christmas decorations. Not out of disrespect, but really, what are you supposed to do with tin canisters with stickers of your cats' names on the lids?

Lara didn't like it. Her cats had loved being with her, sleeping against her, sitting on her lap, distracting her from reading. The thought of them relegated to the cold dark garage just didn't sit well. And now she had a better option for them.

Lara hated having to open up the perfectly crafted replicas, picking carefully at the belly seams, but she had little choice. She had to trust her instincts.

She'd dumped the ashes into the velvet bags and tucked each bag into the appropriate tummy of the stuffed cats, nestled in the soft poly stuffing so if you squished the cat, you couldn't feel the bag of remains. Cremains, she'd heard the ashes and bits of bone called.

She then neatly sewed up the seams. Grandma DeeDee, who always tried to teach Lara how to sew, would've been proud of her workmanship.

Her mom never missed the ashes, the canisters.

And after that...it was like her cats were with her again. In her dreams, at least, dreams she would remember more vividly than ever before. Pecan, she learned, had no regrets about her roving ways, even though her life was cut short. Her sweet chirps encouraged Lara to explore different paths in her dreams. Biss taught her empathy. Be kind to those who others spurned. He could turn nightmares to sweet dreams of generosity and mercy.

And Brulee? He still spoke to her, late at night, just as she was falling asleep, his not so melodious voice dear to her. He trotted alongside her in her dreams, a slender cat with a big heart, ready to protect her against any nightmares.

"They're coming with me," Lara told her mom. Even if she could bear to be parted from her cats, she knew they'd end up in a box, in the closet on the top shelf or even back into the cold garage, if she didn't keep them safe with her.

And college, halfway across the country, at UT Texas in Austin, was a big step for Lara. She needed them with her. Needed their love and encouragement. Even if it was all in her head, just an emotional construct.

Her mom pursed her lips, but said nothing, placing a flour sack flower garden quilt, Lara's favorite, the first Grandma had ever made her, into the box.

The cats came next, then Lara's favorite squishy pillow on top.

They would be safe on the three-day drive from Torrance to Austin.

———

"I BET we could still get you in the dorms," Lara's mom Julie said, as they pulled up in front of the big white clapboard house. It looked like it should be on hilly acreage, surrounded by oaks and cedar trees, a farmhouse on a *farm*, not tucked into an eighth of an acre lot in an old city neighborhood a mile north of campus. The short grass of the manicured front yard was still brown from the summer heat. Boxwood trimmed into short rectangles framed the bottom half of the big first story windows.

Her mom fretted. "It's so *far* from campus. And you're going to be lonely."

Petite and blonde, her mom looked like the perky sorority sister she had been twenty-odd years before. Lara, with her curly red hair and awkward, angular body, looked nothing like her. She looked like her engineer dad. She had all his social graces (or lack thereof), and his knack for computers, and apparently, since she'd chosen Texas, far from Los Angeles, his wanderlust.

"I'm fine here," Lara said. "It's cheaper than the dorms, and I want private." She had applied to rent rooms at a few places scattered in a one mile radius around campus, studying online maps and rental sites, but this house seemed near-perfect. She'd sent a personal letter, handwritten, to the owner, Mrs Jacobs, hoping it would sway the odds in her favor.

Apparently, it did.

Lara would have one of the two second story suites, with use of the downstairs kitchen and other common areas. She didn't want to share a bedroom, or put up with the chattering of a roommate, in the close confines of a dorm. Just her and her cats in her own space. Just what she wanted. Where she could study and learn without interruption.

"I just worry about how you're going to make friends—" her mom started.

"I'll be *fine.*"

They offloaded Lara's suitcases and boxes, sweating in the late August humidity.

"I'd forgotten just how sticky it can be," her mom said. She sneezed. "And the cedar fever. Certainly didn't miss that." She had graduated from UT Austin herself, twenty years ago. Had met Lara's dad here.

Her mom's allergies were legendary. Their house was decorated and furnished to accommodate her constant wheezing. Bare floors, blinds instead of curtains, leather and wood furniture. HEPA filters in each room. Moving to California hadn't gotten rid of the allergies.

Just gotten rid of the husband.

Amazing that she hadn't been allergic to the cats.

Or was willing to tolerate them, regardless.

"Key's supposed to be under the mat," Lara said. "And an envelope inside with the key to the upstairs suite."

Her mom dug under the welcome mat, rough brown coir painted with blue bonnets, and snagged the key. "Not very safety conscious."

"*Mom!!!*" Lara took the key and opened the door. Felt a quick jolt as she stepped through, like someone checking her identity against a list. The old oak floorboards creaked, like the house was talking to her. It was over a hundred years old, Mrs Jacobs had told her.

Lara bet it had a lot to say.

The stairs to the second floor were right in front of her. A formal dining room with an oak pedestal table, dining chairs, and a built-in hutch, was off to the left, and beyond that, the kitchen; the living room was to the right, with a limestone fireplace taking up most of the far wall. A modern gray velvet sectional and loveseat were arranged around a worn pine coffee table. Cut flowers, yellow and red freesias, adorned the tables. Their heady scent filled the air.

Right next to the door was a small table. She picked up the envelope with her name on it. Another slight shock. Static electricity? But she was standing on wood floors, not even on a throw rug.

"Not bad," her mom said, peering over her shoulder. "And air conditioned. Let's get your stuff in before all that cold air gets out."

They both grabbed boxes and headed upstairs.

Her suite, basically half the top floor of the house, was to the left up the stairs. It was big enough for three separate areas. At the back, with a window overlooking the backyard, a full sized bed (already made up, with ivory sheets and a denim duvet), a tall maple-veneered dresser, and a small closet occupied about half the room. In the center a worn olive green chenille loveseat and a dinged-up small coffee table provided an area to just relax. Two windows with diamond shaped panes illuminated the center of the room. Finally, an old oak desk and chair, set up under the window that looked out over the front yard and street, would be for work and study. White sheer cotton panels dressed all the windows, bright against the ivory painted walls.

She'd have to get some heavier drapes for privacy, at least for the front window. She'd ask the owner if there were any, folded away somewhere.

The bathroom had a toilet, a pedestal sink, and a Pepto-pink tiled built-in shower. The pink continued halfway up the old plaster walls, with black tile edging the top and bottom. Bright white towels hung off tempered glass rods. The chipped white hex tile floor with black hexagons arranged in an abstract floral pattern just added to the vintage vibe.

More freesias, this time pink, sat atop the back of the toilet tank.

"At least it's clean."

"It's *original*, Mom." Lara loved it, chipped tiles and creaky floors and all. She quickly unpacked her box. Tossed the pillow onto the bed. Took out the three cats.

Her mom sighed and went to retrieve more boxes.

Lara looked around the room. Where to put the cats? Biss would be nervous in a new place. She put him on the dresser, closest to the bed, where he'd feel close to her. She felt, rather than heard, his soft purr.

Pecan should go by one of the windows. Pecan would be so excited to see a new place, new street, new houses. One of those big leafy trees across the street might even be her namesake. Lara placed her on the desk, pleased by Pecan's excited chirps.

And Brulee? He would sleep with her, at least this first night. More for her than for him, but he always wanted to take care of her. She'd let him. She placed him on her pillow. For once, he was quiet, satisfied.

And Grandma's quilt...for now, she would drape it over the back of the loveseat. A place of honor. The faded patchwork flowers brightened the olive green of the couch, blended with the esthetic of the room.

She unpacked the box her mom had brought up. Sneakers, sandals, and ballet flats in the small, cedar-lined closet. Workout gear, running shorts, tank tops, sports bras, filled one drawer of the dresser.

Everything fit, it seemed, as she and her mom unpacked the rest of the gear.

And the cats felt content, the soft rumbles of their purrs vibrating against her.

———

HER MOM DROVE them to a nearby grocery store, Central Market. It was huge, with several different restaurant options, as well as an amazing cheese counter. Lara didn't think she'd be able to afford the fancy stuff all that often, but it was here when she could.

"We'll get you all stocked up," her mom said. They had lunch, then shopped, then it was time for her mom to drop her off at the house and drive down to San Antonio to meet up with an old college friend before heading back to California.

Lara would be on her own. The semester—her first semester at college!—would start in a week.

Just her, and the cats, and her whole future.

———

She didn't meet Mrs Jacobs til several days later, days Lara spent exploring the neighborhood (Hyde Park, she discovered, one of the older neighborhoods in Austin) and the UT campus.

Lara learned to run early in the morning, just as the sun's rays touched the treetops, when the moisture rich air was still cool. Her feet thudded against the asphalt to the crow of an illegal rooster in someone's backyard.

She told Pecan and the others everything: about the Tudor house three doors down, with its sweet-smelling rose garden; about the small golf course a few blocks away that housed at least one armadillo she'd seen trundling about; and the campus itself, mostly modern buildings and so big, more sprawling than she expected.

Brulee would listen, too, but Biss was happy indoors, not worried about the outside world.

She registered for her classes. Explored the campus. Bought her textbooks.

In the evening, once the sun set and the bats had flown out from under the Congress Avenue bridge, she walked a mile each way from the house on Avenue F to Central Market, just to grab a sandwich, hunker down at a picnic table, and listen to whatever band was playing in the courtyard.

Tejano, rock, country, it didn't matter. What mattered was that she somewhere new, ready to start her life. Experiencing whatever the city would offer.

She was just unlocking the front door one night when she finally met Mrs Jacobs. She truly hadn't known what to expect: the woman seemed efficient, even brusque, in their communications prior to Lara renting out her suite. But then the flowers had been such a nice touch. And they were definitely for her; no one else had moved into the suite across the way.

Mrs Jacobs was tall and slender, with long silver hair tied back in a ponytail. Her eyes were ice blue, undimmed by age. She wore a chambray shirt, heavy turquoise-studded silver bracelets, a flowing khaki cotton skirt, and tooled black cowboy boots with red and blue floral insets.

Hopelessly chic, the deep lines on her tanned face only giving her character. If Lara's cheerleader mom made her feel awkward and gangly, this elegant woman utterly cowed her.

Lara's skin tingled, little zaps of electricity raising the hairs on her arms.

Then Mrs Jacobs smiled, a broad smile that shattered the iciness in her eyes.

"Welcome, my dear," she said, shaking Lara's hand firmly. "It's so good to finally meet you. Your cats have told me so much about you. Especially that Siamese. He just doesn't know when to stop talking, does he?"

———

Mrs Jacobs sat Lara down in the living room. The scent of freesias still hung thick, but warm cinnamon and vanilla seeped from the kitchen.

"Hold tight," Mrs Jacobs said. "I'm going to make some coffee. And I have some coffee cake I baked earlier."

Lara sat on the edge of the gray velvet sectional, hands on her knees, knuckles white.

Her cats had always *seemed* real, not just stuffed replicas of her beloved pets. More real than she admitted was healthy. And she knew her mom worried about her, worried how attached she was to the cats.

And she thought they talked to her. In her dreams, right before she awakened. At night, if she was reading a book or coding an app, really into it, she could hear Pecan's little chirps, Brulee's strident calls, Biss purring softly.

Mrs Jacobs returned with a tray holding two slices of cake, streusel topping spilling off the plates; two mugs of coffee; and an antique creamer and sugar bowl pair, silver tarnished to a warm gray.

"You have no idea what you did, do you," she stated, arranging her skirt and slouching against the back of the loveseat, kitty corner to Lara.

Lara shook her head. She picked up a mug, added some cream, then sipped, nearly spilling it all over her t-shirt, her hands were shaking so much. It was rich and bitter and hot.

"You think everything is a problem to be solved. Computer science, right?"

Lara nodded.

"I'd say cat got your tongue, but you look like you're close to passing out and won't appreciate my puns. Have some cake, my dear."

"How...how can you hear them? Is it real?" Lara asked. "Are they real?"

"Neat little bit of necromancy you performed," Mrs Jacobs said. "Now, put that fine mind of yours to work. Tell me why you're here."

"I'm going to study computer science."

"Not here in Austin. Here in this house. How did you manage to get a room in this fabulous old house, in one of the nicest neighborhoods in Austin, for such a ridiculously low price?"

"I wrote a nice letter?"

Mrs Jacobs sighed. "Your saliva on the envelop practically sparked power. I didn't even care what you'd written, though you are more eloquent on paper than in person. So, yes, the letter."

She leaned forward, blue eyes intent. "I have a responsibility for training young witches. That second suite will likely be filled before the end of the week, with another gifted youngster."

"But-—"

"Do you understand how lucky you are that your cats are good, noble creatures? That you had only the purest of intents when you worked your spell? You don't even know you created a spell." She jabbed a finger in Lara's direction. "That is why you are here."

"For me to learn."

"Yes! Not just at the University, but from me. And you will work hard, both there and here. Are you ready for that?"

Her cats *were* real? Her cats were *real*?!

And she did that?

"Yes," Lara said. "I've always been ready."

DOWN TO THE HEART

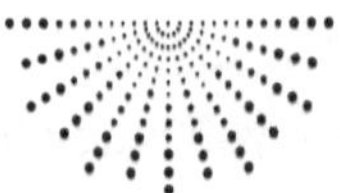

Jennifer tugged on her wetsuit, shimmying her hips as she pulled it past her thighs. She tried hard to use her fingertips, not her blunt nails, but she could feel the soft sleek neoprene rip as she yanked. The wetsuit was an Orca tri suit, a man's wetsuit because the women's sizing didn't go big enough. Even this, a 3X, wasn't made for her Rubenesque curves, baggy at the waist and tight across her hips and breasts.

The transition area, racks loaded with fancy carbon fiber bikes, running shoes lined up just so, towels and kitty litter pans with fresh water in front of the bikes, was empty except for her. Everyone else was lining up in their age groups on the beach, splashing in the waves to get used to the cold Pacific. 66 degrees, the race officials had announced.

Once the pale October sun came up, it'd get warmer, but not enough to matter to any of the triathletes.

Why ever would someone name a wetsuit brand Orca? She felt big enough as it was, never mind encased like a plump sausage in the snug black wetsuit. She reached for the strap hanging off the zipper and tugged. It pulled up partway.

She could ask someone in her wave, her age group, to help, when she got down to the beach.

Triathletes were nice, right?

Awake at 3:30 a.m., she'd driven the hour to Malibu and parked, unpacking her bike, Rocket Bike, and her tri bag, full of her gear, by herself. She set up her transition zone like she'd practiced. She'd gotten body marked by a bright eyed high school volunteer, her race number inked onto her arm, calf, and thigh.

And then her gut roiled so bad she didn't think she could hold it during the long wait for the port-a-potty. She just wore her tri top, a tight tank top, and lightly padded tri shorts. She didn't think she could manage her wet suit in the confines of the port-a-potty.

Diarrhea. She'd used the last of the toilet paper, with a mental apology to whoever came after her. At least she hadn't gotten anything on the floor. Seemed like other people weren't so careful. She was too big, too awkward to hover over the seat, like she expected most of the other athletes had done. She'd just sat her ass down on the seat after giving it a wipe with the second to last seat cover. The last seat cover she'd placed on the floor, for her bare feet.

By the time she'd left the port-a-potty to get her wetsuit on, there was no one else waiting for a toilet.

She headed down for the beach, zipper strap flapping against her goose-pimpled back. The first waves had already started. A sea of orange heads bobbed just past the surf, heading out to the first buoy two hundred yards offshore, followed by a clump of kelly green barely visible in the churning white water of the shore pound.

Her own swim cap was gold, along with all the other Athena athletes in her wave. She'd wavered between signing up for Athena (women over 140 lbs) and her age group, but the Athena wave started before her age group, and she figured there was less chance of her being the last person on the course if she started the race earlier.

The coffee she'd gulped on the way still coated her nerves-dry mouth.

Except for the volume she could feel stretching her bladder.

She joined the group of women with gold caps. Most had water beaded up on their tri suits. She wished she'd had time to get into the water before the race.

"Can you zip me?" she asked a woman near her.

"What?" yelled the woman. Her swim cap was pulled tight down over her ears, the strap of her goggles looped behind her skull and the googles themselves perched on her head.

Jennifer snagged her zipper pull, wagged it.

"Oh sure! Turn around. Pull your shoulder blades together." The woman pulled up the zipper and tucked the pull under a neoprene flap. "There you go. First time?"

Jennifer nodded. Was it that obvious?

"You'll do fine!" the woman said. "I'm Roxy. This is my fifth tri. Just do your own race. Don't worry about anyone else."

"I think I have to pee," Jennifer said. She did. Why was her bladder screaming at her *now*? She'd just spent a half hour stuck in a port-a-potty.

"Just pee in your wetsuit. Urine is sterile, everyone does it, yadda yadda," Roxy said. "Plus, it'll warm you up." She flashed a toothy smile.

An airhorn blared and the group ahead of them entered the water, splashing into the breaking waves until it was deep enough to start swimming. Jennifer glanced back up the beach to the port-a-potties. No way was she going to make up back up through the soft sand and to the port-a-potty, get her wetsuit off, get her wetsuit back on, and back down to the water's edge to start the race on time.

Her wave would leave in five minutes.

Her bladder spasmed.

"Just do it," Roxy said, smirking.

She did. Once past the momentary shame, the *wrongness* of it, she felt better.

Like a real triathlete.

Good thing, because that's when the airhorn went off for their wave.

———

CHAOS. Utter chaos. Hundreds of women jostling, splashing, shoving to get into the water and headed out away from shore.

Well, not hundreds, probably just around fifteen.

Jennifer hung to the back and outside, letter the faster, more experienced athletes out in front of her.

Even so, her goggles got knocked askew just as a huge set of head-high waves barreled in, the biggest set of the morning.

She clutched her goggles in one hand and held her right arm held out in front of her, closing her eyes (she was wearing her contacts) and gulping air and sea spray as she dove blindly under the wave.

She didn't dive fast enough or deep enough.

The wave tumbled her around.

Opening her eyes wouldn't do a darn thing in the shore pound of the Pacific, the water being more sand than water with the force of the waves churning up the sand.

Someone kicked her legs, another person kicked or hit her head. Other people caught in the wave or just oblivious. She knew it wasn't personal, but right now it seemed like everyone was conspiring to drown her.

Which way was up?

Sunlight glinted through her squeezed shut eyelids, but another wave rolled her, bashing her face against the ocean floor. A gush of warmth from her lower lip mixed with the bitter saltiness of the ocean.

Her chest ached. Burned.

How did it get so deep so fast?

Which way was up?!

Strong cold hands grasped her upper arms, and Jennifer realized you could shriek underwater.

Garbled, and it used up the last bit of air in her lungs, but identifiably a shriek.

"Relax, you idiot," a sibilant voice hissed at her.

And she couldn't help it.

She opened her eyes.

A freaking *mermaid* had a hold of her.

And not some pretty, frou-frou teenager with a shell bra.

The water was crystal clear, Tahiti-turquoise, so she could see every detail.

This creature looked positively carnivorous, with huge black eyes, iridescent scales patterning across its narrow face, and hair that looked like glowing long slender sea anemone tentacles.

And its teeth...it had the teeth of an angler fish, jagged and slender and pointy.

Perfect for shredding flesh.

And it brought that face close to hers, closer, closer, til those hard fishy lips were pressed firmly against hers.

And blew air into her mouth.

Granted, fishy tasting air, but air.

Jennifer sucked it in, feeling her chest relax.

A freaking *mermaid*.

"Can you finish?" it asked, moving back just a little, but keeping hold of Jennifer's arms. "Finish the race?"

Jennifer nodded. She wanted to finish it. Had to finish it. Had to prove to herself that she could.

To show all the people who told her she was too fat, too slow, obviously too undisciplined. Because how else would she look like she did?

Most of all, to prove it to herself, that all those people were dead wrong.

"Good. Start kicking," the mermaid said, and *shoved*.

———

UP WAS *UP*.

———

THE WATER CHANGED, from clear to sandy, and Jennifer burst through the waves, sucking in a deep breath of fresh air. She could see the buoy ahead, see gold swim caps shining against the sea. She tucked her head down and swam, long efficient strokes with her arms, rotating her body back and forth, gently fluttering her legs, reserving those for the upcoming bike and run. She actually caught up to someone from her wave, swimming around the first buoy. A race volunteer, balanced on a longboard, cheered her on.

The second buoy was a quarter mile ahead, but she was in her groove, stroke stroke stroke breathe, rinse and repeat. She rounded that buoy, and paused, stopping to tread water. To look at the shore.

And the waves slamming into the beach.

Her stomach clenched.

She'd have to time it just right, catch a wave and let it carry her, not fight it.

She could do it. She had to.

She tucked her head down and swam. Fifty yards, a hundred, and she could feel the swirl of the currents. She glanced back over her shoulder, gauged the incoming set of waves. Swim a bit more, feel the swell, then *GO!*

She let the wave carry her along. It felt like flying. Just her, the sea spray, and the immense wave beneath her like an orca gathering itself for a leap.

At least til she scraped up on the beach.

———

SHE SLOGGED up the beach in a daze, kicking the soft dry sand, unzipping her wetsuit and yanking the top half down as she ran, just like she'd practiced a dozen times over.

Where was Rocket Bike? Head down the middle, halfway down plus a couple more rows, and there it was. Her bright red aluminum Trek that she bought used on Craigslist, and loved more than any car she'd ever owned.

She stepped in the kitty litter pan, rinsing the sand off her feet, then yanked the wetsuit the rest of the way off. Toweled off her feet, shoved them into her bike shoes, attached her race belt with her number, then it was all go go go!

She had water bottles in cages on her bike frame and electrolyte chews like oversized gummi bears in her top-bar mounted Bento box. She swished some water in her mouth while leaving the transition area to the main road, rinsing the salty bloody taste and spitting.

All she had to do was clip-in to her pedals and hit the hills. The hills weren't crazy, not like the ones she'd trained on, climbing for miles on every weekend since last November. These were just rollers. Feel the burn pedaling up, then click to the biggest chain ring and let her thighs, her wonderful strong powerful thighs, add even more speed to the downhills, enough to get her halfway up the next roller without even breathing harder.

Shoot, she could even gawk at the Malibu mansions, what she could see through the gates as she rode by. Maybe even see someone famous.

At least admire the ornate stone, iron, or wooden fences, and the roadside landscaping. Breathe in the sweet heady scent of dry sage. Enjoy the cherry flavored electrolyte chews. Rehydrate.

That worked for about eight miles, all the way out to the turn-around point and back a few.

Less than five to go.

Then she crested the biggest hill yet, clicked to the biggest ring, began pushing, and ran over *something*. She didn't even know what. A rock? A crack in the asphalt?

It didn't matter, because when she skidded and reflexively hit the brakes, the bike stopped and she didn't. She fell over, scraping up her legs, the road rash burning, sliding along for several feet.

It felt deeper than road rash. Blood washed the road grit off her knees.

Oh, god, did anyone see that? The fat girl crash on her bike?

"I saw," a gravelly voice said from the side of the road. A man sat under an oak tree, with a vintage Indian motorcycle parked in the shade of the oak. He stood up and stomped over.

He was short, with a bald head already sunburnt from the morning sun, and a beard that reached his knees.

He looked like a motorcycle-riding dwarf straight out of diesel punk Tolkien, complete with a black leather jacket, worn jeans covered by leather chaps, and fingerless leather gloves.

"I can help you," he said. "Looks like your wheel got bent. Or you can just wait for someone else to come along and take you back to the finish line, if you'd rather not do more.

"If you'd rather just quit now."

The wheel of her bike *was* bent. She would need a new wheel, and even for her entry-level bike, those weren't cheap.

And she certainly couldn't ride on it.

"You can fix it?" she asked. "Really fix it?"

"If that's what you want." He glanced at his thick fingernails, began digging grease out from under them. He stank of motor oil and mud and sweat.

"I do," Jennifer said.

She had to do this. She had to finish. She was more than halfway through, and the thought of giving up now...she couldn't. Wouldn't. If she had the choice....

He nodded, then reached for her bike. Ran his scarred hands over it. Nodded again, approvingly.

"He's really sorry," he told her. "Didn't mean to fail you. Knows you've taken good care of him up til now. Not your fault."

"Rocket Bike," she whispered.

"Yep," he said. "He likes the name." The man reached for the front wheel. "This might hurt," he whispered to Rocket Bike. "But you'll feel better after." He gave a quick wrench, muscles bulging along his fore-arms, and straightened the wheel.

Rocket Bike didn't even let out a squeak.

"Here you go, Lady," the man said, handing the bike to Jennifer.

She clipped in and rode like the wind.

No. Not like the wind.

Like Rocket Bike had real rocket boosters and the ignitors had kicked in.

———

THE RUN WAS a simple out and back along the concrete path, then along a dirt road. Ocean on one side, dirt and rock cliffs on the other.

She tossed off her bike shoes, placed Rocket Bike reverently onto the rack, then pulled on her running shoes. She didn't bother to rinse her scraped and cut knees, but she did carefully apply Body Glide to her inner thighs and underarms. Looked like deodorant, but it would keep her inner thighs and upper arms from getting a huge painful rash from chafing.

She took the time to drain a water bottle dry. Volunteers manned the turnaround point, a mile and a half plus away, with cups of warm water and encouragement, but she needed to rehydrate *now*.

She ate another electrolyte gummi, too. Strawberry this time, the sweetness giving her extra pep.

Just a 5k to go.

And she wasn't the last person. That wasn't the most important thing, and she felt bad even thinking it, but darn it, no one wants to be last.

Especially the fat girl everyone assumes *will* be last.

She jogged out of the transition area.

Just a 5k....

———

JUST A MILE TO GO. One stinking mile.

Nearly back to the concrete path, beach and ocean on one side, parking lot on the other. Shoot, she could see her sky-blue Prius, fifty yards ahead.

And her foot slipped. A rock, a ridge in the dirt, who knew.

Her ankle wrenched and she fell, so hard she couldn't catch her breath for a moment. Then pain shot up her leg.

She could feel her ankle swelling.

She tried to stand, collapsed. Sucked in another breath. Yeah, that was it. She wasn't sobbing. Nope.

She could hobble to her car. Maybe. Drive it to the transition area, after everyone had left. Get Rocket Bike. Go home. Forget about all of this.

What was she thinking?

Why did she ever think she could do this?

Mermaids, dwarves, who gave a shit?

"Are you really ready to give up?"

A rabbit. A talking rabbit. Long ears, a fluffy white tail. Powerful thighs and big paw-feet, made for running.

Jennifer snorted. Sobbed. Sucked in more air.

It had antlers. Not just a rabbit.

"A *jackalope*? Shit, what I need is a freaking unicorn with a healing horn," Jennifer said.

It studied her dispassionately. "Well, you've got me," it finally said. "And yourself.

"If you want to give up, I'll help you get to your car," it continued.

"And if I want to finish, you'll fix my ankle? Help me finish?" Jennifer said.

"No. You have to do that yourself." He lifted a long rear foot to his mouth, began grooming his stubby claws. "Get your own self to the finish line. But, if you want to quit, I'll help you get to your car. Even help you get your stuff. Rocket Bike, right?"

"Fuck you," Jennifer said. "I hope you get fleas."

She scrambled up. Her ankle hurt like hell, but it wasn't broken. She could do this.

She had to. She was too close to give up now.

She limped towards the finish line, the jackalope hopping just a few steps behind her.

The whole last mile.

———

"NUMBER 697, CONGRATULATIONS! You are now a triathlete!"

Jennifer flung both her arms into the air. She didn't know if she was laughing or crying, but as she ducked her head for the volunteer to hang her finisher's medal around her neck, she knew she earned it.

And it wouldn't be her last.

———

A VOLUNTEER WRAPPED up her ankle for her. The swelling had gone down, and the stabbing pain had subsided. She had a bottle of ibuprofen in her bag, so she popped a few, chasing them with a whole bottle of water and a couple slices of oranges. She grabbed a bagel, too, poppy seed. Tasted better than any bagel she'd ever had before.

Mermaids. Magical dwarves. Jackalopes. Who knew if that was all just her brain playing tricks on her. Oxygen deprivation. Pain.

But when she got home, when she unloaded Rocket Bike, checking the front wheel one last time, she noticed something.

The front wheel was now carbon fiber.

Not aluminum.

THE MONKEY'S JOURNAL

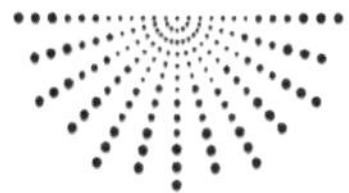

Kelly stroked the cover of the worn paperback. *Song of the Fateful Stars*, by one of her favorite authors, Mary Lobos, who'd died, oh, about fifteen years ago.

Song of the Fateful Stars was long out of print, and Kelly hadn't read it in more than ten years, since she loaned her copy to someone she used to consider a friend, and never got the book back. This one was a first edition, with the original artwork, swirling silver stars against a black velvet sky. It was more expensive than she could afford, but oh, she wished she could take it home.

She hadn't thought this little bookstore that she'd just discovered, tucked between a laundromat and a Thai restaurant in a brick building that should have been condemned fifty years ago, could get any better.

But it had.

The whole store smelled like books—not musty, just like dried paper and leather, with a faint overlay of citrus wood polish. The bookcases that stretched along each of the walls and in rows down the middle of the store gleamed, the oak warm in the yellow overhead lights, fixtures Kelly thought original to the 1920s building. Exposed brick walls extended above the tops of the bookcases, and the plaster ceiling was gently coved.

And the books! Everything from mass market paperbacks at half the cover price, to pristine 1st editions lovingly stored in archival sleeves.

Like this one.

"Do you have a good heart?"

Kelly turned.

The proprietor of the tiny bookstore stood in front of her, other side of a low wooden bookcase filled with first editions. A ginger cat wove between her legs, purring like mad.

The worn waxed pine boards of the store floor hadn't even creaked under the proprietor's steps.

Every time Kelly shifted, the floor squeaked.

The proprietor had long grey hair collected in a bun, anchored with two number 2 pencils, the erasers worn to nubs. Her face was gently lined, like the cover of a well-loved leather edition, but her cheekbones hearkened to Hitchcock blonde loveliness. Her piercing gray eyes under neatly plucked brows just added to that. She wore a navy cashmere pullover over trim khakis, and put Kelly to shame with her elegance.

The scent of tea roses, delicate and floral, just as elegant, wafted over to Kelly, mixing with the smell of old books and leather.

Elegant would never describe Kelly. She felt especially grubby today, her own long mouse brown hair pulled back in a curly, tangled ponytail. She wore snug faded torn jeans, scuffed navy sneakers, and a cream Aran sweater with a hole in the elbow she meant to darn.

And she was chewing a stick of spearmint gum that had long lost any flavor.

Classy. Real classy.

"Do you have a good heart?" repeated the proprietor.

"I'd like to think so," said Kelly. She didn't kick puppies or pinch small children. She donated to several charities as often as she could, with money saved from her meager income as a barista. She fed the small clowder of stray cats (and had painstakingly captured each, and had gotten them all neutered) that lived in alleyway behind her rented mother-in-law apartment, in the backyard of an old 1920s Tudor mansion.

The only time she did anything *mean* was to the characters in her not-yet-published novels.

Them, she tortured, with a fiendish delight.

"I love that book," the proprietor said, pointing at *Song of the Fateful Stars*. "I knew Mary. She had a good soul. Never acquired the popularity she deserved, not even after I tried to help her. But that was her choice, and she was happy with it.

"You're a writer, too, aren't you?"

Kelly nodded. "I am."

It had taken her eight years to own that. Four years of undergrad, two years getting her MFA, then the past two years. She'd had a few short stories published, but had yet to sell any of her novels. But she *wrote*, and that's what made a writer, right? Writing and learning and reading? Telling stories?

"I can tell," the proprietor said. "I can always tell. That's my gift."

The proprietor walked around the bookcase and back up to the front of the shop, and reached under the glass topped counter. She pulled out a journal, with a burnished saddle tan leather cover and bright red bookmark ribbons.

"This is for you," she said.

"Um, I just keep track of everything with an online calendar," Kelly said. "It's lovely, but I have a very small house, and I've never got into that Bullet Journaling trend..."

"And you are terrible at accepting gifts. It's your choice, of course. But I would recommend you take it. Use it to write about your dreams. Your desires. What you would like to see happen."

Kelly hesitated.

"You can have that copy of *Song of the Fateful Stars*, if you take the journal," the proprietor said. "A second gift."

The little sticker on the plastic bag said $45.

She couldn't say no to the offer of the book, but....

"It's too expensive," she said.

"It's *my* choice," the woman said, arching a slender eyebrow, holding out the journal.

Kelly took it.

———

BY THE TIME Kelly got home, the sun was setting, a riot of smog-stained scarlet and orange. Say what you would about Los Angeles, the smog made some pretty sunsets, especially in the winter.

The littlest cat in the clowder, a tuxedo female that Kelly had named Callista, sat on the coir door mat (emblazoned with *BEWARE: Writer in Residence*) in front of Kelly's door, her left paw held up. It looked swollen.

"Oh, Calli," Kelly said, crouching down, a few feet away from the little cat. "Let me see?"

Calli glared at her, then limped into the jasmine bushes. Kelly couldn't blame her. Last time Calli had let Kelly close, Kelly had swooped her up, tucked her into a crate, and taken her to the vet to get spayed.

She'd check on Calli tomorrow, after work.

Kelly set her sneakers neatly by the door, and the canvas tote she used as purse, with *Song of the Fateful Stars* and the Journal safe inside, onto her dinged-up Craigslist coffee table.

Tea. She needed tea. Jasmine, her favorite to drink while curling up with a book. She'd write later, but now she wanted to read.

She brought the pot of tea, fragrant and floral, to the coffee table, along with her favorite mug:

*Piss Me Off, You Die**
**in my next book*

She had a couple regulars at the coffee house that she wished she could show that mug to.

Only reason *one* guy hadn't been banned was because her manager Ken was too afraid of bad reviews.

This guy leered at the female baristas and mocked the male baristas. Kelly was sure he was the one who pissed in the men's bathroom sink, once, when he didn't get his order (a large pour over with two shots of espresso, light dairy free whip, and a dusting of cocoa powder in the shape of a heart, the drink order also known as The Asshole) quickly enough.

Well, worry about work tomorrow. She poured herself a cup of tea, settled onto her couch (secondhand Ikea, off white duck slipcover, also Craigslist, story of her life), pulled her daddy's old kelly green and amber Pendleton blanket over her legs, and thumbed to the first page of *Song of the Fateful Stars*.

Her eyes drifted to the leather journal.

She had accepted it. She should use it.

She set her book down, and picked up the journal. It felt heavy. Solid. She opened the cover, the leather soft and warm under her fingers. The journal was refillable: pockets on either side held the interior notebook snug. The pages of the notebook were thick ivory paper, with faint gray horizontal lines, bound to the lightweight interior cover. A pen was tucked inside, one of those fancy Japanese markers. She uncapped it, and wrote the date in the upper right hand corner of the first page. December 16th. The brown ink of the pen matched the leather. Nice.

I received this journal today from the owner of the Sunset Books, she wrote in her messy cursive. *I don't know quite what to do with it, but I truly believe I shouldn't have anything in this tiny home of mine that I don't use. So I better figure something out, even if it's just a glorified diary.*

I didn't catch her name, but she looked like what I'd imagine Marion Crane would look like thirty or forty years later, if Norman Bates hadn't murdered her. So I'll call her Marion.

Marion said to use it to write down my dreams and my desires.

I don't have any extravagant dreams. I'm pretty happy as is. I mean, we'd all like to be a success in our chosen field, right? But it seems silly to write down fantasies. Unless it's one of my stories, lol.

Kelly paused. LOL? Well, it was her darn journal. She could write whatever she wanted.

Anyways, my desires...I wish Calli could learn to trust me. I wish she wasn't hurt.

That's it for now.

———

KELLY HAD OVERSLEPT, staying up late to re-read *Song of the Stars*, finally turning off her bedside table lamp at 3:12 a.m.

And then she'd tripped over Calli, laying on the door mat, on her way out, wrenching her ankle. The tuxedo cat rolled over and waved her white paws at Kelly, a sweet expression on her little round face.

Calli's paw looked fine. Slender and dainty, not swollen.

Kelly didn't have time to think as she hobbled to her car, an old Prius she kept running with prayers.

She had to get to work.

Thankfully she wasn't the six a.m. opener, but she knew Mark, who *was* opening, would be desperate for Kelly's help by now. Kelly clocked in at 6:59, one minute early, and just stood still for a few seconds, inhaling the happy bitter smell of roasted coffee beans. Yeah, it was just a job to pay the rent, and her back ached by the end of her shift, but she really did love coffee, loved interacting with the clientele, loved the people watching when the morning rush slowed and the screenwriters camped out.

She pulled herself an espresso that she downed in five seconds flat just for the caffeine, and took over the register.

Mr Asshole was in line, and visibly upset, his cheeks ruddy and his eyes narrowed. His hair gleamed silver. He wore a suit, expensive, Kelly thought, and was tapping his highly polished designer shoes. If he wasn't such a jerk he'd be fairly attractive, for an older man.

Scratch that prior thought. She loved interacting with *most* of the clientele. Not all.

Too bad she hadn't been ten minutes late. She would've missed him. But Mark didn't deserve that.

"Good morning, Mr Jensen!" she said. "The usual?"

"What do you think, you over-educated brainless twit?"

Kelly kept a bright smile fixed on her face. He'd be gone in five minutes.

"I've seen you here the past three years. Guess you don't have enough talent to get out of this dead end job."

She'd memorized his order, "the Asshole". Large pour over , two shots of espresso, light dairy free whip, and don't even think of forgetting the dusting of cocoa powder in the shape of a heart.

A heart. He didn't deserve a heart. Probably didn't have one. She sprinkled cocoa randomly across the dairy free whipped cream and capped the drink. Her own small act of rebellion.

He took it. Then took off the cap. Looked at it. Sneered.

And leaned over the counter and dumped it over her head.

"You fucked up my order," he said. "Make it again."

Oh, god, that hurt. It was fucking *hot* and all she could do was not scream as she reeled back. Her sore ankle flared with pain, and she stumbled back from the counter.

Everyone was looking at her, all the people in line, all the people sitting at the tables. Her cheeks flamed.

Hot coffee trickled down her cleavage under the neck of her t-shirt, settled against the band of her sports bra.

Mr Jensen, Mr Asshole, smirked at her. Smirked.

Mark ran to her like he was in a horror movie, limbs moving, face twisted in fear, but not making any progress to Kelly.

"Make it again, you stupid bitch. And make it right this time."

"Fuck you!" Kelly screamed, gripping the counter. Tears welled up, making her angrier. "Fuck you, you asshole!"

Mark reached her, wiping her face with a cold water-soaked towel. It burned, raw against her face.

"That's assault," Mark said as he patted at Kelly's face. "I'm calling the cops."

"Go ahead," Jensen said.

"I've got it all on video," one of the patrons, a regular, said, waving his phone in their direction. "Posting it now."

Jensen turned. "I'll get you for defamation, asshole, if you post it."

"Go ahead," said the guy, standing. He was big, over six feet, with a physique that screamed personal trainer.

"Better just leave, *now*," Mark said. "Kelly, are you okay?"

Her face was puffy, hot to her fingertips. "Not really," she whispered. "But I will be."

Jensen snorted. "I'm taking my business elsewhere." He left.

"Good riddance," the guy said. "Seriously, Kelly, I've been getting coffee here for a couple years now. You're a great barista. A great girl. If you need the video, just let me know. And I think everyone here would be a witness, if you decide to press charges."

Murmurs of assent from the surrounding patrons.

"Want me to take you to Urgent Care?" Mark asked.

"Don't have enough spare cash for the deductible," she said. "Can I have another towel?" She'd weathered enough coffee burns. Cool it down. It didn't feel like anything was blistering, yet, and it all hurt like hell, so the burns weren't too deep. Hopefully. She silently thanked her thick curls.

"Actually, um, care if I just stick my head under the sink?"

———

SHE FINISHED HER SHIFT, taking a shirt featuring the coffee house's logo from the sale bin to wear and coiling her damp hair into a loose bun at the nape of her neck. By the time the manager, Ken, got there a couple hours later, and she realized she might be able to get medical care under workman's comp, her face and head were feeling better. Her ankle even felt better.

Just the normal throb in her skull and legs and back from a busy morning.

Mark dumped out the tip jar. "Take it," he said.

She looked at the pile of bills and coins. Nearly three times what they normally got in tips.

"We split it. Like always," she said.

"Nope. You suffered for this cash." He shoved it at her. "Buy one of the good bottles of wine at Trader Joe's."

She couldn't argue with that logic. At least not the suffering. She'd skip the wine. The cash would go into the fund for the clowder's care. Maybe she could catch Calli and get her foot checked out. It couldn't have gotten better just overnight.

By the time Kelly parked her car in the alley behind her home, she was second guessing herself. A bottle of wine might not be such a bad idea. But she had to write. Better if she had a clear head.

Calli waited for her on the door mat. She sat primly, equal weight on both front paws, green eyes calm.

"Mrow." She had a husky voice for such a tiny cat. She stood and wove between Calli's legs, purring.

Kelly reached down and gently, tentatively stroked her little round head. Calli had never, ever, let Kelly pet her like this. Kelly held her breath, but Calli just purred louder. Then walked off under the jasmine bush, not limping at all, with a last sassy twitch of her fluffy tail.

———

KELLY SHOWERED, getting the last bits of cocoa and coffee out of her hair. Her face didn't look too red, and she didn't see or feel any blisters.

She'd gotten lucky.

She sat at her desk and opened her laptop. She was currently working on a new novel, second in a trilogy, about a young witch in training. She loved young adult, YA. She could get as deep into controversial topics as she liked, but it was also okay to keep things light.

She opened her document. Hesitated. Then grabbed her journal. She had to write about today, get it out, get out all the rage she'd kept bottled up her entire shift, with the exception of her initial outburst.

Jensen had smirked at her.

Jensen didn't care that he could have seriously injured her.

He enjoyed that he could get away with hurting her.

Kelly had no doubt Jensen would call Ken at some point, frame it all as her fault (granted, she didn't do a freaking *heart* on his drink, but....), and end up getting free drinks for a month that she'd have to serve him with a smile.

Unless she quit.

Dipped into her savings, and threw herself into writing full time.

She couldn't quit. What if she had been seriously hurt? She needed more of a financial cushion.

She opened the journal, clutched the pen.

Mr Jensen AKA Mr Asshole freaking poured coffee on me today.

I wish he would get smashed by a truck. Or a bus. And die screaming.

———

SHE WAS READY FOR CALLI, purring and rubbing against her legs, the next morning.

"What's gotten into you, kitten?" Kelly asked, scritching behind Calli's ears.

"Mrow!"

Kelly laughed. Add cat treats to the shopping list. She had to stop at Trader Joe's after work, anyways. If Calli continued warming up to her like this, she'd check with her landlord Mrs Kronenberg to see if she could officially have a cat.

She got to work at her normal time, 6:45 a.m., enough time to make herself a flat white and to enjoy it before clocking in.

She had just finished, the whole milk and espresso coating her mouth, when she jumped and stumbled, her ankle flaring with pain, even before she registered the screech of the tires and the whine of the brakes of the LA Metro bus.

And the screams, the agonized screams so shrill she thought someone was smashing a spike into her skull.

Until the screams stopped, and Kelly stood up from where she'd fallen, ankle flaring with pain.

Mr Jensen had been hit by a bus. Died screaming.

She'd killed Mr Jensen.

———

I KILLED SOMEONE TODAY.

He was awful but I didn't really mean to kill him.

Her head hurt so bad she just wanted to cry. And her chest. It was like someone had punched her in the sternum, hard.

Or like she'd been hit by a bus.

Please bring him back. I wish he hadn't been hit. I wish he wasn't dead.

———

HE STAYED DEAD. At least, he didn't show up at the coffee house.

Kelly considered maybe that wasn't the worst option.

She had dreamt of him dragging his broken, bleeding body into the coffee house, the body that shouldn't be alive, but shambled up to the counter.

"Give me my regular, you murdering cunt," he said, blood dripping from his mouth, his chest and abdomen crushed. "And don't forget the fucking heart. Mine's like a piece of pounded beef."

No. He stayed dead.

At least, she thought, for now.

Of course the bookstore was closed, steel shutters pulled closed over the front facade.

She went around to the back, pounded on the metal door until her hand ached as much as her ankle and her chest.

Pounded until the proprietor of the bookstore opened the door and raised a thin elegant eyebrow.

"You should have told me," Kelly said.

"Told you what?"

"About what the journal was. It's a freaking monkey's paw."

"Stray cats get better, or they die. They learn to trust, or they remain feral. And sometimes, people get hit by buses. Sometimes it's something people have secretly hoped for. It doesn't mean anything,

Kelly. Except how you feel about it all. How you feel about yourself and what you wanted."

"Take it back. I don't want it anymore."

The proprietor shrugged. "There's nothing more it can do. Keep it, child. And know: I still think you have a good heart.

"The question is, do you think you do?"

ABOUT THE AUTHOR

Since graduating from West Point, Stephannie Tallent has served in the Army as a Military Intelligence officer during Desert Storm, gotten a Zoology degree, went to vet school, worked as a small animal veterinarian, and designed and published knitting patterns and books.

Throughout all that she's always wanted to be a writer, and she's finally put all her type A, soft-spoken, invisible middle-aged woman focus on that goal, writing everything from fantasy to science fiction, mysteries and romance.

She has sold stories to Pulphouse Magazine and the WMG Holiday Spectacular.

www.stephannietallent.com

Sign up for Stephannie's newsletter!
https://www.stephannietallent.com/subscribe/

ALSO BY STEPHANNIE TALLENT

Short Story Collections

Gates of Wonder

The Chronicles of Dinah Lee Wright Vol 1

The Chronicles of Dinah Lee Wright Vol 2

Gratitude of the Ocean: Jolene Tomberlin Series

The Serpent in the Shallows: Jolene Tomberlin Series

The Monkey's Journal

The Kaleidoscope Jaguars of the Jungles of Mexicatl

The Mermaid of Ellis Prime

The Alchemy of Science and Mystery

One Plus One Equals More (mystery/crime)

A Snowman Made of Sand (romance)

KnitWitch (fantasy and knitting patterns)